I0654688

Mary Elizabeth Herbert

A Saint In Algeria

Mary Elizabeth Herbert

A Saint In Algeria

ISBN/EAN: 9783337299576

Printed in Europe, USA, Canada, Australia, Japan

Cover: Foto ©Andreas Hilbeck / pixelio.de

More available books at **www.hansebooks.com**

A SAINT IN ALGERIA.

BY

LADY HERBERT.

(Reprinted from "The Month.")

LONDON: BURNS AND OATES.

1878.

A SAINT IN ALGERIA.*

THERE are few visitors to Algeria who do not make a pilgrimage to the beautiful basilica of " Notre Dame d'Afrique," either for purposes of piety or to see the glorious views from the mountain on which it is placed.

Probably few of the former leave the place without stopping for a few moments at the little shop or stall which abuts on St. Joseph's Chapel, and where, accord-

---

* To conform to the laws of the Church, the writer declares that, in this biographical notice, she only uses the name of " Saint," or speaks of revelations and miracles, in the sense in which it is permitted to do so, while humbly submitting all judgment on such matters to the Holy See.

ing to French custom, a multitude of pictures, medals, crosses, and photographs of
" Notre Dame d'Afrique" are to be sold.
But to those who frequented this stall in
past years, one of its great attractions was
the sweet face and winning manner of the
lady who sold those little objects of devotion.

Now that the grave has closed over
the earthly remains of this humble but
saintly woman, we venture to give our
readers a short account of her life, drawn
from authentic sources, to which, through
the kindness of the Father Superior of
Notre Dame d'Afrique, we have had
access.*

Margaret Bergésio was born in Piedmont, at Conio, near Turin, in the year
1809, on the 8th of September, the feast
of the Nativity of our Blessed Lady, that
Mother whom she so devotedly loved,

---

* The greater portion of the facts in this biographical notice is taken from a series of articles in
the African *Revue de St. Augustin et de St. Monique*,
signed " L. J. Christus."

and to whose honour she was hereafter to contribute so much.

She was an only child, for her father died soon after her birth, and her mother having married again, the little Margaret was intrusted to the care of her grandparents, who were models of virtue and practical piety. They devoted themselves to training the heart and soul of this little child ; and the seeds of faith and holiness sown by them were to bear fruit hereafter a hundredfold. Yet they were only allowed this consolation a short time, for their grandchild was but eight years of age when her mother determined to leave her native country and settle in Lyons, on which occasion she insisted on taking her little girl with her, having no children by her second marriage. Bitterly as her grandfather felt this separation, he was happily unaware how terrible the change would be to poor little Margaret. There is in those quiet villages of Piedmont a manly earnest piety, an unquestioning faith, and a tender reverence for all holy things, which stamp a peculiar character upon its inhabitants. It is the same atmosphere as is felt, even by Protestants, in the Tyrol. Our Lord and His Church form the main points, so to speak, in their daily lives. Every house, every field, is placed under holy protection, and to miss Mass on days of obligation or to neglect Easter duties would be an unheard-of sin, visited by the reprobation of the whole community.

In this sort of religious atmosphere had the little Margaret been trained, and we can therefore form some idea of the feelings with which she suddenly found herself transplanted into a big town, where every one was a stranger to her, where no one seemed to think of or care for our Divine Lord and His Mother, and where all the pious practices of her childhood were ridiculed and contemned. Her mother was her greatest trial. Utterly frivolous and worldly, and without any religious principles herself, she embittered every hour of her child's life, and all the more as, with the strong feelings of filial reverence which had been implanted in her, Margaret did not dare remonstrate or argue with her mother, even on certain points in which she knew she was right. It was indeed a special grace which preserved the poor child's faith at so tender an age from the effects of her infidel surroundings. But it does not appear that our Lord ever allowed the smallest doubt to sully this pure and virginal soul. Thwarted in all the religious practices in which she most delighted, and exposed to the reproaches and ridicule both of her mother and stepfather for what they called her " prudish ways," Margaret only suffered in silence, and, whenever she could, escaped to her little room to cry and pray. Even her name was changed by her mother to please her new French friends, and the child was henceforth known only as Agarithe Berger. Then began her tender devotion to our Lady of Sorrows. She had a little picture of the Seven Dolours, which her grand-

father had given her, and, young as she
was, she daily united her sorrows to those
of Jesus and Mary, and endeavoured at
their feet to gain strength and wisdom for
her difficult path. No wonder then that,
when she presented herself, by stealth, at
St. Nizier, in Lyons, to be prepared for
her First Communion, the holy priest to
whom she came for instruction was amazed
at the precocious intelligence and piety of
the child, who answered all his questions
with a degree of spiritual knowledge which
edified as much as it surprised him.
Agarithe was then eleven years old, and
to the last hour of her life she would
reckon among her most signal graces
having at that time fallen into the hands
of a director who so thoroughly understood the wants of her soul, and who
could discover the precious treasure which
it had pleased God to conceal there. He
guided her through all those sad and
difficult years (of which Agarithe never
could bear to speak), when childhood is
merging into girlhood and girlhood into

womanhood, with all its pecular trials and temptations—increased, in her case, a thousandfold by her painful domestic circumstances. She was not quite twenty when (in 1829), disgusted with the world, of which she had long since found out the deceptions, she obtained leave from her mother (with great difficulty, as may be supposed) to enter the community of Nursing Sisters (*Sœurs Hospitalières*) in the Hôtel Dieu at Lyons. She was then in the full beauty of youth, with a gentle loving manner, and a peculiarly modest, sweet expression ; but over her face, from the very beginning of her childish sorrows, a look of resigned sadness had been cast, like one who is an alien from her real home, and that expression remained on her face till death.

Happy indeed were the days she now passed in the hospital. She seemed to have found her vocation in every sense of the word, not only from her love of solitude and recollection with God, but also because the rest of her time was spent in tending the sick, the poor, and the miserable, towards whom her whole heart had always gone out in love and compassion, as for the suffering members of Christ's body.

Yet it did not please Him that she should be allowed to spend more than one short twelvemonth in this house. God had other designs in store for her. The revolution of 1830 brought a complete change in the administration of the hospital, and the open hostility and ill-will of the new managers of the institution compelled the chaplain to resign. He was also the director of the Sisters, who felt that it was impossible to remain in an establishment where they could no longer observe the rules of their order. The community was therefore broken up and the Sisters dispersed. But Agarithe always gratefully expressed her sense of the obligation she was under to those religious for the training in poverty and holy obedience she had there received.

An event happened about this time

which had a great bearing on her future
life. This was the appointment of M. Pavy,
then quite a young priest, to be the vicar
of the church and parish of St. Bonaventura
at Lyons. It was while seeking out the
lost sheep among his numerous flock that
this holy pastor first discovered Agarithe's
mother; and thus he became acquainted
with her holy and devoted daughter, who
henceforth chose him as her director and
guide. Finding her most anxious to undertake some work for God, he placed her
first in a kind of work-room, where he
had gathered together some fifteen or
twenty young needlewomen, under the
superintendence of a very holy woman
named Mdme. Aulinet, who had the reputation of directing her little household like
an austere religious community. All pious
exercises were here performed at stated
hours, and the employments of each day
were so marked out that, between and after
the hours of work, the members undertook
to go by turns and carry food or clothing
to the poor, to visit the sick, to serve the

bedridden or blind, and to pray in the
name of the rest before the Blessed Sacrament or at the feet of Notre Dame de
Fourvières on the hill above the town of
Lyons.

Two years of Agarithe's life were spent
in this holy home, of which she ever retained the most affectionate remembrance.
She used often to recall those days, and
laugh over her nights, which were spent
in a long drawer by way of a bed, placed
on some planks in a raised corner of their
common sitting-room ; so anxious was she
to preserve her vow of poverty, and not
to take anything from the feeble resources
at the disposal of the house, which were
mainly devoted to the relief of the suffering poor around them.

She only left this place in obedience
to her confessor, who wished her, with
another companion, to undertake a fresh
work, and that was a home for young
workwomen and apprentices without
parents or proper supervision, who were
to come back to her for their meals

and for the night, and whom she was to look after and encourage in every possible way to persevere in the right road. The number of souls thus saved by her winning ways and gentle influence is known only to God.

But our Lord was not content with thus employing her in His service. Perhaps to one of her active zeal and fervent temperament such work was only too attractive and too happy in its visible good results. He Who destined her to reach the higher paths of perfection, led her by a hidden way of suffering, for which she was totally unprepared. He sent her a long and dangerous illness, and the trial was heightened by the unkindness of her relatives and by the utter destitution to which she was reduced. The Home had to be given up, and she and her faithful friend, who never left her (Mdme. Anna Sinquin), removed to a little room in a poor house near the church. Here for fifteen years she lived in a condition which outwardly had nothing remarkable about it; but which in reality became a source of inexhaustible merit to her, from the terrible and varied sufferings she there endured and the perfect union of her will to the will of God. Being entirely incapacitated from labour of any sort and quite confined to her bed, Anna went out to work to earn the food of both; while Agarithe was left the whole day long entirely alone, without any of the alleviations her suffering state required, and exposed to every kind of privation. She had the grief, likewise, of seeing her charitable efforts to save the souls of those young girls brought to a close, and the Home, from which she had hoped so much, shut up and abandoned. Yet her faith and love never failed. " To suffer, therefore, is what awaits thee, if thou art resolved to love Jesus and constantly to follow Him." These words of the *Imitation* were ever present to her mind; and, as Fénélon justly says, that " where there is no resistance of the will there is no suffering," so her simple acceptance of what to others appeared so insupportable a cross, brought with it not only resignation but cheerfulness and even joy. She resolved to offer up a portion of her sufferings for the conversion of her mother, who was getting old and infirm, yet as far as ever from God. And this offering was accepted; so that Agarithe had the inexpressible consolation of seeing her mother return to her childhood's faith and die in 1840, fortified by all the rites of the Church. Soon after this happy event, Agarithe's health began slightly to improve, which enabled her once more to have the joy of hearing Mass and even to visit Notre Dame de Fourwières, the sanctuary for which she had such special devotion. Her love of solitude, her union with God in the Blessed Sacrament, her devotion to Mary, and her willingness to suffer as long as it was the will of God, continued to increase. At last, satisfied with her acceptance of this heavy trial, our Lord removed it as suddenly as it had been sent, and Agarithe recovered both health and strength. This was the moment chosen by God for the commencement of the work to which He had appointed her, and for which her previous life and sufferings had been the preparation.

It was in 1846 that M. Pavy was appointed to the episcopal see of Algiers. At the first news of his promotion, Agarithe's heart sank within her; for he had been her director, guide, and faithful friend for seventeen years, nor did she then see the smallest prospect of meeting him again on this side of the grave.

One of Mgr. Pavy's first cares on arriving at Algiers was the establishment of a Seminary, wherein he might train priests for his enormous diocese, as well as native missionaries for the evangelizing of the Arab tribes. But no sooner had he obtained a house for this purpose, than he found that everything was needed for the fitting up of the establishment; and that, what was more important than all the rest, was to find some conscientious person to take charge of the linen of the house and to have the care of the infirmary and the sick students.

His first thoughts naturally turned to Agarithe and her companion, and he wrote at once to implore them to join him in Africa. Agarithe regarded this request of her spiritual father as an answer to her prayers and a direct order from above. She and her friend at once made the necessary preparations for leaving Lyons; and braving the dangers of the sea and expatriation, which to French people is more terrible than to any other nation, they arrived in Algiers less than three months after their beloved Bishop and guide.

He at once put Anna in charge of the house; and to Agarithe, who had served her noviceship at the·Hôtel Dieu as Hospital Sister, he confided the care of the infirmary. Few of the Algerian priests who were trained in the Seminary of St. Eugène during that time have forgotten the motherly and tender care of their Infirmarian when laid low by the fever and other diseases, which seem inseparable in a hot climate to the fresh comers from a more northern land. But all made one remark : and that was, that during the eight years Agarithe held this office, not only did her devotedness never fail, but that extraordinary cures were effected when the doctors had given up all hope. Not one death took place at St. Eugène during her residence there; and the students ascribed this fact less to her remedies and good nursing than to the efficacy of her prayers.

Agarithe herself soon began to look upon Africa as her adopted country. But one thing alone grieved her in leaving Lyons, and that was, no longer to be able to climb the steep hill which led to Notre Dame de Fourvières ; that holy sanctuary where every Saturday of her life at four o'clock in the morning (when not incapacitated by illness) she had offered up the prayers, the praises, the sufferings, and the good works of the whole week to the Mother of Consolation. Nothing in

Algiers replaced this privation, and the longing for it only increased as years rolled by.

It was full of these thoughts that Agarithe, during her few moments of leisure, used to wander in a little valley near the Seminary, called " The Ravine."

It is a narrow valley completely hemmed in by rocks, through the centre of which a rapid river flows over moss and stones, here and there falling in little cascades and running eventually down to the sea. By the side of the river and following its windings, runs a little path shaded by fine old olive-trees. The banks on both sides are carpeted with flowers and evergreen shrubs, interlaced with honeysuckle, clematis, and other creepers, forming a delightful shade, even on the hottest day. The whole place speaks of peace, recollection, and calm.

This ravine was one of Agarithe's favourite haunts. Unhappily it became also a hiding-place for vagabonds of all sorts; so that Agarithe soon found it impossible to find there the much-loved solitude she sought for.

She was pondering over this one day, when she received the sudden inspiration to place a little statue of our Lady in one of the forked branches of one of the old olive-trees which shaded the path, and to establish her there as Mistress of the Ravine. She felt as if she had received a direct order from Mary to cause her name to be honoured in this mountain, which had been formerly watered by the blood of martyrs. Agarithe communicated this idea to the Bishop of Algiers, who warmly approved of it; and that very day the inspiration was carried out, and a little white statue of Mary came to take possession of a mossy throne which had been prepared for her close to the path, in a spot where the vegetation was the most luxuriant and the flowers the brightest. Agarithe arranged it all and then went home joyfully, persuaded that our Lady would henceforth preserve this spot from all evil.

Her confidence was not misplaced : from that day forth the ravine was no longer the rendezvous of rogues, but became the scene of constant prayer. Some sailors' wives had remarked Agarithe, when going along the path, devoutly kneeling at the foot of the little statue and praying with a wonderful expression of love and fervour. This unexpected sight impressed them all the more when anxious themselves for the safety of those they held most dear. On stormy days, or when a severe gale had passed, they took the habit of coming up to the ravine, either to invoke our Lady's protection or to return thanks ; and some would bring flowers, others candles, and burn them at her feet.

Agarithe's heart overflowed with joy at these manifestations of piety and love. She foresaw that this mountain would become a place of pilgrimage like that in her beloved Lyons, and Mgr. de Pavy, who shared in her regrets for Fourvières, saw in this humble beginning an indication of what the future would bring forth, and determined to make the Blessed Virgin the patron of his immense diocese.

Very soon, the number of pilgrims and the graces obtained by them increased so much that Agarithe once more had recourse to the Bishop; and with his assistance a grotto was built of rocks and shells, and a more suitable image of our Lady was brought there by the Bishop himself (accompanied by all his clergy and students), who solemnly blessed the statue and took possession of the spot, while hymns in our Lady's honour and verses composed for the occasion were sung by the whole company.

Yet even in the midst of her joy, Agarithe was not satisfied. She wanted to build a larger and more permanent temple on that mountain, which should be, as she called it, the " Lighthouse of Africa"; but resources of all kinds were wanting.

At last, Mgr. Pavy determined to build a provisional chapel, trusting that his successors would be enabled to complete what he had begun; and on the 2nd of July, 1854, the first stone was laid of the new building.

It was then arranged that Agarithe should leave the Seminary and take up her abode in a little house adjoining the chapel, both to promote the devotion to our Lady and to sell tapers and other pious objects, the profits of which were to go towards the expenses of the building. From that day until the close of her life she never left this poor cabin or the work which the Bishop had assigned to her.*

Much anxiety, many hindrances, and many difficulties arose to retard the progress of the building. But Agarithe never lost heart : she seemed to have a conviction that the work was one which God, in His own good time, would both bless and enlarge. At last the chapel was com-

---

* Such was her love of solitude and retirement that for ten years she never went once down the hill to Algiers, although this town is only at the distance of three kilomètres from Notre Dame d'Afrique.

pleted. But where could they find a
fitting statue for the sanctuary?

Now it happened that when Mgr.
Dupuch (Mgr. Pavy's predecessor) was
passing through France on his way to his
new diocese of Algiers, the ladies of Lyons
offered him a magnificent statue of our
Lady in bronze, on condition that it should
be placed in the first church built on African soil in honour of the Blessed Virgin.
This statue was placed at first by Mgr.
Dupuch above his own palace at Algiers;
but the Government interfered, dreading
lest this newly-conquered people should
take offence at so Christian an emblem.
He then gave it to the Trappists at
Staouëli, who placed it above the entrance-
gate of their monastery, with the inscription:—

POSUERUNT ME CUSTODEM.

It was this statue that Mgr. Pavy went
to the Trappists to reclaim, saying: " You
have made this Madonna the guardian of
your house. Well, now I want her to

change places and become the Queen of
Africa." The Trappists replied that they
could not refuse her to the Bishop; but
also that they had not the heart to take
her down themselves from her place as
guardian of their monastery. The Bishop
smilingly said " he would see to that," and
the next day sent workmen and a cart to
transport her to the mountain chapel.
Agarithe joyfully received her new Queen;
and surrounding her with flowers and
lights, watched over her with all love and
honour until the moment came when she
was solemnly installed above the altar on
which Mgr. Pavy was about to offer the
first Mass of the Pilgrimage.

That day an unexpected honour was
paid to the humble Agarithe. At the
moment of administering Holy Communion, Mgr. Pavy looked around, and not
seeing the Foundress of the Pilgrimage
among those who were kneeling at the
altar rails, paused and called her by name
in a loud voice, amidst the crowd of
priests, religious, and pilgrims of every

class who filled the sanctuary. Agarithe was, as usual, kneeling in a little corner at the furthest end of the chapel, and intending to be the last guest at the Eucharistic Feast. But at the voice of the Bishop, she was compelled to come forward; and thus his humble penitent was the first to receive from his hand the Holy Communion at the first Mass of the Pilgrimage of Notre Dame d'Afrique.

It was on the third Sunday in September, the feast of our Lady of Seven Dolours, that this first Mass was celebrated. And the date rested in Agarithe's memory, not only from her tender devotion, from a child, to our Lady's Sorrows, but because she looked upon it as a prophecy. " Notre Dame d'Afrique will henceforth be the consoler of all sad and broken hearts!" she exclaimed, when that evening the Bishop came to rejoice with her over the success of her undertaking. And her words have indeed come true; for not only the Catholics of Algeria, but Christian mothers throughout the world have there an association of perpetual prayers, which have obtained endless graces, and wiped away countless tears!

But the devil could not bear to witness the success which attended Agarithe's efforts to wrench away from him a kingdom which had so long been his own, and to place it in the hands of her who was to " bruise the serpent's head." On the 10th of March, 1860, as Agarithe was kneeling alone before the Blessed Sacrament and the statue of our Lady, absorbed in prayer, a fearful storm burst over the mountain, uprooting the trees, and carrying off the roof of the chapel, while all its ornaments, sacred vases, and everything it contained, were scattered to the winds. The statue of our Lady alone remained immovable on its pedestal. The violence of the storm may be judged by the fact that the foot of the monstrance was found at the bottom of the mountain, and its rays on the top! The Bishop, much alarmed for the safety of Agarithe, hastened, as soon as the wind would allow him, to the spot. He found her chapel in ruins; but she herself stretched on the pavement safe and sound at the feet of our Lady. Agarithe was always convinced that this fearful tempest was Satan's last farewell to a spot which for so many years he had made his own; but on which the "Morning Star" had now risen to enlighten and guide the people into all truth.

The zeal of the pilgrims soon repaired the damage done by the storm. Money and gifts for the altar poured in on all sides. And then again Agarithe opened her heart to the Bishop, imploring him to build a larger and more worthy sanctuary on this spot. "See the crowds who cover the mountain top," she would exclaim; "only a few can enter in and kneel for a moment at our Mother's feet. Think how faith would grow, how many graces would be obtained, could we raise a temple large enough to contain all this multitude!"

Mgr. de Pavy agreed; but added, "that he had no means whatever to undertake any fresh work." Agarithe, with the

lively and simple faith of the saints, turned
to a little statue of St. Joseph and said :
" He was on earth the Procurator of the
Holy Family. He laboured and toiled,
by the sweat of his brow, for thirty years
to provide them with necessaries. I can
never believe that he will turn a deaf ear
to us now, if we ask him to help us to
make a fitting home for Jesus and Mary !"
The Bishop, moved by her earnest words,
gave her his blessing, and told her to
begin praying at once.

Agarithe instantly placed a picture of
St. Joseph in her little shop, before which
a lamp burnt continually. Among the
works she had placed under St. Joseph's
patronage was the distribution of a quan-
tity of little pious books and prayers,
which she gave gratis to the pilgrims,
exhorting them to take them away as a
remembrance, and to read them in their
own homes to their families. This means
she now made use of to spread far and
wide her appeals for help to build a larger
church. And St. Joseph rewarded her

confidence in him far beyond her expectations. She soon brought a comparatively large sum and laid it at the feet of Mgr. Pavy. "Here are the first stones, Monseigneur!" she exclaimed. "I implore you to begin the work, for I am quite sure St. Joseph will find us the means to finish it."

The Bishop joyfully assented, and resolved to build a temple worthy of its object, to be called, henceforth, Notre Dame d'Afrique. Plans were drawn up; a committee appointed to see them carried into execution; while the Bishop wrote himself to France in all directions for aid in this gigantic enterprise. His appeal was warmly responded to, and the work rapidly proceeded. But the holy old man did not live to see its completion. He died, watching from his window the white cupolas of the beautiful basilica already surmounted by the cross, and recommending to the veneration of his clergy the holy woman who had been the real Foundress of the building.

It was in the month of November, 1866, that God called Mgr. Pavy to his rest. He was succeeded by the Bishop of Nancy, Mgr. Lavigerie, who became the first Archbishop of Algiers. Agarithe's prophecy was about to be fulfilled, and the sanctuary of which she had been constituted the special guardian was soon to be crowded, not only with her country-men and countrywomen, but with Mussul-man children, who would learn to lisp their prayers to " Imana Mariam," as they called her, and finally become true cham-pions of the faith of Christ.

WE need not dwell on the horrible famine which, during the very first year of Mgr. Lavigerie's episcopacy, spread its black pall over the land. His charity and its results are well known. Suffice it to say that, when every orphanage and his own palace were full to overflowing, he brought the remainder of these poor children to his villa at St. Eugène, under the shadow of "Notre Dame d'Afrique," which became henceforth as "Holy Land" to them. The frequent pilgrimages and processions to this magnificent shrine struck them no less than Agarithe herself, whose greatest delight was to lead them to our Lady's feet. Sometimes they would ask those who superintended them "whether this lady who was always praying was not really the angel sent by heaven to guard the temple?" In fact, the extraordinary beauty and sweetness of her expression struck all visitors to the church, while her profound recollection awed them too much to let them intrude upon her devotion.

It was about this time that the Holy See delegated to Mgr. Lavigerie, in addition to his diocese of Algeria, that enormous tract of country called the Sahara and Soudan, comprising upwards of fifty million pagans; and the indefatigable prelate at once resolved to found a special missionary congregation for this work, comprising both men and women. On the 2nd of February of the following year the first four missioners who had come in answer to his appeal met him at Notre Dame d'Afrique, where the Arab dress was given them. The eldest of them likewise received that day sacerdotal consecration from the hands of the Archbishop, and was the first priest of the new congregation. Everything was done privately and in silence at this touching ceremony, and no one was permitted to be

present but Agarithe, who, after the ordi-
nation was over, came joyfully and kissed
the hands so recently anointed, and then
kneeling asked for his blessing, adding—
" You are the first priest to wear this
dress, but you will not be the last, for God
has blessed this grain of mustard-seed, and
before long this chapel will be too small to
contain the number of those whom our
Lord will choose to labour for the salva-
tion of our poor Arabs."

Her prophecy was verified even in her
lifetime, for in less than eight years this
congregation numbered one hundred and
thirty missionaries devoted exclusively to
the evangelization of North Africa.

No sooner was " Notre Dame d'Afrique "
completed, than Mgr. Lavigerie invited
a religious community (of Premonstratensians) to undertake its services ; but
they only remained three or four years.
Great as was Agarithe's joy at the care of
the church and pilgrimage being intrusted
to so fervent a body, this appointment
became, in the designs of God, an occasion

of the severest trials she had ever known, and of a kind to which she had hitherto been a complete stranger. When God wills to possess a soul altogether, He does so by immolation. He sends the suffering to which that soul is the most sensitive, and it is through that channel of intense pain that He gives Himself the more abundantly.

We have seen how, from her childhood, Agarithe had passed through the crucible of suffering, and we have come to that period in her life when all ordinary pains and sacrifices were only as ladders leading her higher and higher towards Him Whom she loved. The only real joy she had on earth was to receive Him daily in Holy Communion, and then remain for several hours absorbed in prayer and thanksgiving in the silence of the sanctuary, pouring out to Him all the secrets of her heart and soul. Now it pleased God, for her greater sanctification, to send her, in the person of one of these religious, a director who totally misunderstood his penitent, treated her as an enthusiast or a visionary, and imposed upon her one of the most painful sacrifices she could have been called upon to make. That was, to leave the church the moment the priest came down from the altar, scarcely giving her time to make an act of thanksgiving after receiving Holy Communion. Thus poor Agarithe, who, like Magdalene, would willingly have passed her life at the feet of her beloved Spouse, was obliged to limit her prayers to the few instants which elapsed between the giving of Communion and the close of the Mass, and was then compelled to hasten back to her shop. Once there she did not know a moment's peace. The pilgrims crowded round it day by day, besides a multitude of people who sought her advice on every possible subject; so that often she had not a single quarter of an hour to herself till night. This most extraordinary trial lasted five whole years! She owned once that nothing had ever cost her so much; but added, with her usual simplicity—" It was, perhaps, because so few souls have such great need of obedience as my own." But this was not all. This same director, either to prove her, or because God permitted this blindness on his part still further to try the faith of His servant, told her one day that she must leave the place, give up the church and pilgrimage of which she was the foundress, and return to France. He ordered her likewise to join a religious community, saying that he did not approve of the way of life she had hitherto led or the position in which she had been placed.

The blow was an overwhelming one, and became a terrible crisis in a life which was already drawing towards its close. But she persuaded herself that it was her duty to obey, and to accept the trial laid upon her without a murmur. Before leaving Africa, however, she sought the venerable Archbishop, in whom she had the greatest confidence, and who had always been her extraordinary confessor, and told him that she was compelled by obedience to give up

her work at Notre Dame d'Afrique and
return to Lyons. It was then that God
revealed His will to her, and showed her
that, as with Abraham, He was satisfied
with her obedience without exacting the
sacrifice. Mgr. Lavigerie answered without a moment's hesitation—"Return to
your cell. I order you to remain where
you are. I will speak to your director;
but be very sure you will be the last
person that will be allowed to leave
Notre Dame d'Afrique!" The veneration of the holy Archbishop had always
been very great for this chosen soul.
Many times he was heard to exclaim—
"I have known a great many people, and
lived in many different countries, but I
never in my life met with a person whom
I think such a saint as Mlle. Agarithe."
And whenever he bent his steps to Notre
Dame d'Afrique, to implore our Lady's
aid in his gigantic undertakings, he would
stop at her little shop and order Agarithe
to go and pray for his intentions. " Our
Lord and His Mother never refuse her

anything," he would add to those around him, as she hastened away to obey his behests.

We hope we have not wearied our readers by referring so often to Notre Dame d'Afrique and its pilgrimage, but it was, as it were, the centre round which every event in Agarithe's life was grouped, from the hour she first landed in Africa. There the first native orphan children were baptized; there the first of the Arab-Christian marriages were solemnized. There again, in 1873, the first African Council was held, after centuries of desolation and darkness. To Agarithe one of the greatest joys in this last event consisted in the fact that all the sacred music used on that occasion and all the ceremonies, were performed by Africans recently converted to the faith of Christ. It was on that day, too, that the statue of our Lady was finally removed from the little chapel where she had so long been venerated to the magnificent throne which had been prepared for her above the high altar in the great basilica ; while the small chapel which had witnessed so many prayers and graces became, as Agarithe had prophesied, a sanctuary for him whom she always called her "good" St. Joseph, as Patron of the Universal Church.

One thing only now was needed to complete Agarithe's work, and that was the installation of the priests of the African Missionary College on that spot. Often had Agarithe reproached the young missioners for not bringing their orphan Arab charges more frequently to their holy Mother's feet. "You come here too seldom," she would exclaim ; "this is the natural centre of your mission. This will be your future home."

At that time nothing seemed less likely than their removal to Notre Dame d'Afrique, for the Premonstratensians were building a monastery, with every intention of remaining there. But the troubles of 1871 dispersed the community, and then, as Agarithe had foretold, the Society of African Missioners were finally established in their place, and native priests and servers now gladdened the eyes of that holy woman, whose one prayer had been to bring the Arab tribes to Mary's feet.

With the completion of this great work Agarithe felt that her life was drawing to a close, and that she was now ready to sing her *Nunc Dimittis*. Her strength daily diminished ; work of all kinds became painful to her ; her features were drawn and livid, and her mortified body seemed literally to waste away. Her weakness soon increased so much that she could no longer work, but passed her time either before the Blessed Sacrament or in her cell, or in what she called " her little corner," that is, behind the door of her shop, where a little window looked in to St. Joseph's chapel.

" If only death would take me in this little den," she would exclaim, " I feel I should then die better at my post ! " But sometimes she added, " I think I should like best to die while sweeping out the chapel, and so to appear before our Lord with my *arms* and while doing a work so honourable to a servant of Jesus and Mary."

To sweep and clean the church and keep it in the most perfect order, was one of the things she loved best. She looked upon it as the greatest privilege and honour, and would not yield it to another, even the very day when she was compelled to take to her bed. It was the last manual work she ever did.

Her reverence for holy places and things was extreme. When she saw the young Arab neophytes kissing the door of the church, she would joyfully exclaim : " Oh, how I understand these poor children, and how I love to see them show such respect to God's house ! " If any one ever gave her a small sum of which she was free to dispose, she would buy incense with it, saying, " I should like to burn perfumes all day long wherever our dear Lord deigns to come and dwell with us." To a lady who one day complained of acute bodily pain, she said : " Make use of some of the oil

which burns in the lamp before the Blessed
Sacrament. You do not know the healing
virtues which God gives to that precious
oil which honours Him by burning day
and night before His Throne."

Next to her love of our Lord in the
Blessed Sacrament and of the Blessed
Virgin, the devotion which she strove the
most to propagate was that to the Holy
Family, and especially to St. Joseph. In
the very last letter she wrote to an intimate
friend, she exclaims: " Dear——, have
unlimited confidence in St. Joseph. Every
morning I pray for strength and courage
for you to the Holy Family, and especially
to him. He suffered on earth, and he
understands your needs. I have the
greatest confidence that this, his Month of
March, will not close without your receiving
abundant consolations."

This holy woman wrote little in her life,
partly from her wish to remain hidden and
unknown ; partly from her isolation from
the world since she arrived in Africa. But
a few letters, addressed to an intimate

friend, who became a nun, have been preserved, from which we will give a few
extracts.

Writing to her in February, 1843, on
the eve of her departure for the cloister,
she says : " My poor dear friend,—How
much strength and courage you need at
this moment ! But He for Whom you
give up everything will restore to you
what you have lost a hundredfold. You
know Jesus is never outdone in generosity.
Take your heart and soul in both hands,
and with the cross and love of Jesus
Christ break all those chains of human
affection which bury you under their
weight. It is better that you should feel
the whole length and breadth of the sacrifice you are about to make. Your Divine
Spouse will only value your offering the
more, for it proves the ardour of your
love. Well—a heart on fire for God can
do great things.

" Dearest friend,—Let us look on this
world as a great prison, and then we shall
let our Master change our dungeon as He

wills, until it shall please Him to open to us the gates of our heavenly country. If you become a holy nun, as I hope and pray you will, your convent will be but the antechamber of your celestial mansion. Everything that you are about to leave behind you, abandon freely to the care of your Divine Spouse—He will take care of all—and then go forward yourself, boldly, without ever looking back . . . . Let us hope that as we have known and loved each other here below, and only parted at the foot of the Cross, we may meet again borne by this same Cross, on Mount Sion, where there will be no more separations, but joy and delights unspeakable for evermore. Yes, Pauline; let heaven be our rendezvous : it is here that I say to you *à revoir !* ”

For more than thirty years this nun and her holy friend had been separated, and had never even corresponded. It was only in 1872 that this Sister, become Superior of her community, remembering the eminent sanctity of her old friend, wrote to ask the aid of her prayers, and also to beg for her advice in her difficulties. It was certainly not from forgetfulness, or from want of affection, that Agarithe had buried her life in such complete silence, but from a spirit of sacrifice. The following passage in one of her letters to this very friend reveals to us the secret : " I promised our Lord a long time ago never to seek for consolation in creatures. *God alone knows what this sacrifice has cost me !* But as Jesus designed to be jealous of my miserable heart, I did not dare divide its affections . . . . Rejoice, my dear old friend," she continues, "that God has sent you such sufferings of heart. When one has gone through this crucible, how far more tender and sympathizing one becomes towards others! . . . Tell me, now, how you are getting on with your troubles. You know that your sufferings and your joys are likewise mine. *Oh, how good it is to have suffered !* How much better one can enter into the sorrows of others, especially into that anguish of soul which no human words can express!"

Yes—souls: that was the passion of her life; to save souls; to find a soul whom she could raise and strengthen to bear the burden of life and bring it nearer to God. Listen to her apostolic words to this same friend a few months before her death : " Courage, dear friend—courage! do not allow yourself to be cast down. God proportions His grace to our needs. The more we are sunk in the abyss of our own weakness and miseries, the more He encourages us to love and confidence. Confidence! Oh, how sweet that word is to my lips! How I should like to run up and down this sad world, crying out to all who suffer — ' Confidence!' Absolute abandonment of ourselves in His hands Who orders all things right. How much I should like to talk to you on that subject of simply giving oneself up, body, soul, and spirit, to His sweet will! It is so wonderful how God brings good out of evil, even when everything seems lost.

Were I not afraid of sinning against charity, I could relate to you some painful experiences in my own life which yet all turned to good in the end, and now even fill me with joy. Therefore, I should like to bring every soul to feel the most entire confidence in *God alone*, hoping nothing from creatures. Besides, in these days, when, alas! men pray so little, our good God is, I think, more ready to listen to the petitions of those who really love Him, and grants us all we ask, especially spiritual favours."

To this passion for souls Agarithe added an intense sympathy for all forms of suffering. Among the many gifts God had bestowed on His faithful servant, one of the greatest and most remarkable was her power of consoling those who came to her in trouble, and especially when it was a question of their conversion. Her warm heart and her never-failing charity inspired her always to say the right thing, and to suggest that which best suited the circumstances and position of each person with

whom she had to deal. Her memory,
too, was extraordinary. She remembered
people whom she had not seen for years,
with all the details concerning their souls
which they had confided to her a long
while before, so that they had no need to
go over again the history of their troubles.
" I know," she would say, "the difficulties
you had in such and such a matter. Now
tell me how you have been going on."
And thus encouraged, they would pour
out their whole hearts, and rarely left her
without feeling their burdens lightened
and their souls drawn nearer to God.

There was one season in the year when
she seemed always to be filled with a
kind of holy exultation ; that was towards
autumn, when the retreat of the religious
communities and the ecclesiastics began.
" How God is being honoured at this
moment," she would exclaim ; "and what
good will result for the future to innumerable souls !"

When she heard of any lost sheep being
brought back to the fold, she was quite

beside herself with joy. A short time
before her last illness, a person who had
lived a very disedifying life, but who had
been converted by Agarithe's ceaseless
efforts, fell sick and died a holy and admirable death, at peace with God and
man. She came with the greatest eager-
ness to announce the news to her director,
her face beaming with joy. "Now that
our dear Lord has granted me this favour,"
she said, "I must never shrink from any
future suffering." Sacrifices and mortifications of all sorts had in fact become,
with prayer, her daily bread. And whenever she had thus a soul to win she would
redouble her fervour and austerities. Yet
her ordinary life was, what would be
considered even by holy people, most
mortified. She slept upon straw and had
only the coarsest food, never touching
either wine or meat. In the evening her
supper was invariably bread and water
and an onion, which her faithful friend
Anna would prepare for her, or some
other vegetable ; and she preferred this to

the most luxurious food. Yet, according to the evidence of this same friend and companion, her outward mortifications were nothing to her interior ones. To one who so constantly watched this pure and fervent life it was evident that her conversation was far more in heaven than on earth. The mere sight of this calm and angelic face, with its extraordinarily sweet expression, in spite of the shade of sadness of which we have already spoken, impressed every one who came to see her. It was like a ray of light from another world.

A soul so closely united to God, so detached from earth, and living so completely among heavenly things, was naturally favoured with special graces and revelations, in spite of the bitternesses with which her path had been strewed. We have often heard the Archbishop say that very frequently she had spoken to him of important matters concerning the Church which she could only have known by supernatural means. So much so, that Mgr. Lavigerie who always had such con-

fidence in her holiness and wisdom, did
not hesitate to consult her in all difficult
cases, and reaped the benefit of so doing
in every instance. One of those who was
permitted to know the intimate secrets of
this chosen soul, writes: "Our Lord spoke
to her very often; but she never would
reveal it unless forced to do so by obedience. I had many proofs of this. One
day in particular, after Holy Communion,
she fell into a sort of trance, and I insisted
on knowing the cause, as she had told
me she would pray for light concerning a
matter which related to myself. Our Lord
had desired her to confirm me in an important decision which I was about to
take, and of which she knew nothing
whatever beforehand."

She had a distinct revelation of her
approaching death, and spoke of it to
several persons. When in May, 1875,
Mgr. Lavigerie, worn out by a long and
dangerous illness, was about to leave
Algiers for a time and go for a change
to Rome, there to find rest at the feet of

the Holy Father, Agarithe drew close to his carriage, which was taking him down to the port of embarkation, and kneeling, exclaimed, " Bless me, Monseigneur! and deign to ask for a special blessing for me from the Holy Father, for we shall never see each other again on earth."

"It is true," replied the Prelate, blessing her with great fervour; " I feel I am at the end of my mortal course."

"No," eagerly answered Agarithe, "you are not the person in question. You will live many years yet to be the blessing of this vast diocese."

The carriage rolled on; but two months after, when the Archbishop heard of the death of this holy woman, he remembered her last words and then understood their full meaning.

From that moment Agarithe's strength hourly diminished; she could no longer stand or even read, and her time was spent entirely in prayer and meditation. At last, on the 25th of June, her director insisted on her going to bed. Then, to the great surprise of her companion Agarithe asked for a mattress, and when Anna expressed her joy and surprise at her consenting to make use of so unusual a luxury, Agarithe replied : " It is that, if any one comes and sees me on my poor bed during my illness, they may not perceive anything extraordinary about it." So strong, even in death, was her determination to conceal all that might make others suspect her austerities !

During her last illness her sufferings were terrible. It was quite heart-breaking to see the way she gasped for breath, to feel her burning hands, and see the perspiration streaming down her face with the agony of the pain. But she only thought of one thing, and that was neither to say nor do anything which should excite the least compassion in those around her.

" I would not give up my place to another for the whole world ! " she would say to her confessor. Nor did she ever manifest the smallest weariness during the whole length of her illness. She took every remedy offered her with the most perfect indifference. One only disgusted her and brought on violent vomiting. Yet she never refused to take it, and only asked the Sister who nursed her to offer it first to Our Lady of Dolours, after which she could swallow it with less repugnance. What most struck the holy missionary who attended her during her last illness, was her unalterable patience in the midst of the most acute sufferings. He used to come and see her regularly twice a day. In the evening she always asked him for his blessing: " It is my best sleeping - draught," she would smilingly say. Almost every morning he brought her Holy Communion, and her soul all through the night was, as it were, consumed with the holy desire to receive Him. " I shall have my Jesus to-morrow," she would exclaim joyfully in the midst of her agony.

On Wednesday, the 16th of July, the feast of Our Lady of Mount Carmel, her sufferings seemed to increase in intensity.

Those around her thought her end was at hand, and that Mary had waited for that day to fetch her faithful servant home. But she guessing their thoughts, said quietly : " No, not to-day; I must wait a little longer !"

In the night she made an effort to turn, as if to find an easier place in her bed. The Bon Secours Sister who was watching by her said : " I am sure you are not comfortable in that position. Will you not let me turn you round to the other side ? "

" My Saviour was far worse off on the cross," she murmured; " leave me where I am."

And the Sister remarked that she stayed so to the end, without allowing herself the alleviation of a change of position.

The next morning, being Saturday, she sent early for Father Pascal, to make her last confession, and also to ask his permission to renew her act of profession as a tertiary of St. Francis of Assisi, on this

the last day of her life. One of the
greatest happinesses of her existence had
been to make this vow of poverty as a
daughter of the Seraphic Father. Mgr.
Pavy had refused it to her for many years,
partly to purify her holiest wishes by contra-
dictions, and partly because he feared to what
excesses her spirit of mortification might, in
consequence, lead her, and she submitted
to the prohibition with her usual angelic
sweetness. On the death of that Bishop
her desire increased still more; but she
had still some time to wait before her
director would permit her to enrol herself
among the tertiaries. She often said that
that day was one of the happiest of her
life. And the renewal of her profession
as a daughter of St. Francis was the last
consolation which she asked for on her
bed of death, a few hours before she was
to appear before God.

"I never shall forget that pious and
touching ceremony," wrote the Father who
was with her. "After kissing respectfully
the book of rules, she took in her trem-

bling hands the wax taper which had been given her at the moment of her profession. One saw on her dying face an expression of supreme happiness ; an angelic smile rested on her lips. I was so moved and touched that I had the greatest difficulty in repeating the prayers, although I struggled with all my might to conceal my emotion. I thanked and blessed God, Who had allowed me to see with my own eyes how a saint can die."

"I here affirm," continued her director, "that I ever found her closely united to our Saviour Jesus Christ, always anxious to suffer every cross which it might please our Lord to send her, and to suffer thus until the end of the world, if that were His Divine will and pleasure. The continual remembrance of the death of her Crucified Lord made all sufferings light to her. Whenever she heard the Holy Name pronounced, an ineffable joy seemed to light up her face. Even in the midst of the most acute suffering, her heart, burning with love and filled with consolation, seemed to taste already of the sweetness of heaven. Taking her little crucifix in her hand, she would kiss with reverent love the Sacred Wounds of our Saviour and exclaim, ' Oh, how enviable is my lot, how happy I am! How many graces hast Thou sent me, my Lord and my God!' and so on, continually making ejaculatory prayers and uttering words of praise and thanksgiving. This privileged soul did indeed hunger after sufferings of which few so well knew the value."

" The thoughts of death," adds her confessor, " which generally send a thrill of fear and agony even through the minds of the best among us, never troubled in the smallest degree this true servant of God. Agarithe saw the approach of the King of Terrors with a joy and a calm which were inexpressible. She had only one wish, and that was to be united to her Spouse and never again to be separated from Him. I have never in my life seen such serenity in any dying person. Ripe for heaven, she had nothing but disgust for the things of earth. In one word, she lived as a saint and she has died as a saint."

Her union with God increased as death drew near. She spoke no more, and seemed not to notice anything around her. She prayed incessantly, and seemed to be holding continually internal converse with God. Once or twice she raised her voice unconsciously, and they heard her praying for her dear African mission and for the conversion of the Arabs. Again, she would offer all her sufferings for the life of the Archbishop. It was believed that she had made an offering of her own life, so that this beloved and indispensable chief pastor might be preserved to his flock. And, in confirmation of this belief, it came about that the health of that venerable prelate, which for so many months had caused such deep and increasing anxiety to those around him, suddenly and without any apparent reason, began to improve from the hour of Agarithe's death, so that very soon he was able to undertake once more, with renewed strength, the superhuman works which his zeal and charity had inaugurated in his vast diocese.

It was on Saturday, the 17th of July, that this soul, so full of virtues and merits, took flight for heaven, leaving a body worn out with sufferings and austerities, and murmuring to the last the sweet name of Jesus. The Sister of Bon Secours, who had watched for three weeks by this dying bed, exclaimed, "In my life I have nursed many priests, many holy nuns, many very good people, but never did I see such a death as that of this saint-like Mdlle. Agarithe."

Scarcely had the news of her demise become known, than crowds of mourners hastened up to Notre Dame d'Afrique to pray by her venerated remains until the hour of her interment. It was at Biarritz that the Archbishop first heard the news, and he hastened to send orders to have a grave prepared for her in the centre of that chapel, first of Our Lady and then of St. Joseph, where for so many years she had lived and prayed. Until the vault was prepared, the coffin was laid in a corner of the chapel. There, day and night, the piety and veneration of the faithful kept up the most brilliant illumination. An incessant stream of people succeeded one another in praying by that bier; and yet no one seemed able to pray for her soul : an inward feeling appeared to force them to invoke her instead. Popular veneration surrounded, not only the bier, but every corner of her humble home. The greatest anxiety was shown to obtain the smallest thing she had used. Rosaries and crosses were brought to touch the coffin, which was covered with the most beautiful flowers. And it required all the vigilance of the priests to prevent the coffin itself from being cut in pieces, and taken away as relics.

The day of the funeral, which was presided over by the Vicar-General, in the absence of the Archbishop, the crowd was such that not one-half could enter the church. Under the pavement of the little chapel her body now rests, and above it is a marble slab, bearing this inscription :—

Hic, in spem beatæ resurrectionis requiescit

MARGARETA BERGESIO,

Quæ Immaculatæ Virginis Mariæ in templo suo per annos P.M. XX. servam fidelem se constituens, omnibus Christianis virtutibus, humilitate, caritate, pietate, enituit et bonum Christi odorem usque ad finem præ se ferens obdormivit in Domino die XVII Julii, A.C. MDCCCLXXV.

Annos nata P.M. LXVI.

To this touching inscription the Archbishop added the following words :—

Tanti meriti ne memoria intercidat

R. P. D. Carolus Martialis Allemand Lavigerie, Primus Algeriensium Archiepiscopus,

Inscripto lapide consignandum jussit.

The pious concourse of the faithful to this tomb has never diminished. The pilgrims of Notre Dame d'Afrique, before descending the mountain, never fail to go and pray for a few moments on the slab which covers the body of this great servant of God. Father Pascal, whose words we have already quoted, wrote again not long ago : " My conviction is that she will one day be on our altars. Nor am I the least surprised that God is already manifesting her sanctity by miracles." The graces obtained by those who have implored her intercession are very numerous. We will only quote one, a declaration signed and attested by the Superior of the Nuns of the Doctrine Chrétienne, who was one of the first who experienced the power of this holy woman's intercession with God.   .

I hereby declare that I had for more than a year a stiffness in my right arm, in consequence of an accident, which prevented my being able to use it. Every remedy was tried in vain. But having gone to pray by the remains of Mdme. Agarithe on the day of her funeral, I suddenly was inspired to touch her coffin with my bad arm, and it was cured directly, so that I could bend it backwards and forwards. I cannot but attribute this grace to the protection of a soul so beloved of God and so worthy of veneration.

(Signed)   SŒUR MARIE JOSEPH MEYER,
            Religieuse de la Doctrine Chrétienne.

Mustapha Supérieure, August 17, 1875.

Perhaps some day we may be allowed
to make known other favours obtained on
the tomb of the humble but now glorious
Agarithe, and to prove that, even in this
century, and on that poor land of Africa,
so lately given back to the Church of God,
the race of saints is not yet extinct. The
key-note of her life was her love of God,
which enabled her to do the simplest and
humblest duties in the most perfect manner. There are no remarkable events in
this biography. Agarithe's life was one
of trial and suffering, such as we see all
around us—of poverty and toil, of no
repute among men. Yet was she dear to
God and to His Saints, and by her faith,
and love, and perseverance in prayer, she
effected a work which, more than any
other, has given a centre of stability to the
mission in North Africa, where her name
will ever be associated, as the *Foundress
of Notre Dame d'Afrique*, with the labours
of those holy Bishops and Priests who,
by the grace of God, have once more
planted the Cross of Christ on that land,

which for so many centuries had been sunk in Mussulman darkness and error.

NOTE.—Among the graces to be obtained at Notre Dame d'Afrique, there is one which is little known in England, and that is a Mass said in perpetuity every week for the souls of those who have died at sea, of whom a careful list is preserved. It is said at the altar of St. Monica, which has been specially blessed and indulgenced by the Holy Father, who enriched it with the arm of the Saint. Should any mother who has thus lost her boy, or other relative of those who have been drowned, wish to have the names dear to them recorded in this manner, Lady Herbert, of 38, Chesham Place, London, will be happy to receive any such names and offerings, and transmit both to the Father Superior of the Missions there.

THE END.

WYMAN AND SONS, PRINTERS, GREAT QUEEN-STREET, LONDON, W.C.

A

𝔖elect ℭatalogue of 𝔅ooks

LATELY PUBLISHED BY

BURNS AND OATES,

17, 18 PORTMAN STREET

AND

68 PATERNOSTER ROW.

LONDON:
ROBSON AND SONS, PRINTERS, PANCRAS ROAD, N.W.

𝔅ooks lately published

BY

BURNS AND OATES,

17, 18 PORTMAN STREET, W., & 63 PATERNOSTER ROW, E.C.

———o———

Sin and its Consequences. By His Eminence the CARDINAL ARCHBISHOP OF WESTMINSTER. Second edition. 6s.

> CONTENTS: I. The Nature of Sin. II. Mortal Sin. III. Venial Sin. IV. Sins of Omission. V. The Grace and Works of Penance. VI. Temptation. VII. The Dereliction on the Cross. VIII. The Joys of the Resurrection.

'We know few better books than this for spiritual reading. These lectures are prepared with great care, and are worthy to rank with the old volumes of sermons which are now standard works of the English tongue.'—*Weekly Register.*

'We have had many volumes from his Grace's pen of this kind, but perhaps none more practical or more searching than the volume before us. These discourses are the clearest and simplest exposition of the theology of the subjects they treat of that could be desired. The intellect is addressed as well as the conscience. Both are strengthened and satisfied.'—*Tablet.*

'Of the deepest value, and of great theological and literary excellence. More clear and lucid expositions of dogmatic and moral theology could not be found. No one can read these very forcible, searching, and practical sermons without being deeply stirred and greatly edified.'—*Church Herald.*

'His Grace has added to Catholic literature such a brilliant disquisition as can hardly be equalled.'—*Catholic Times.*

'As powerful, searching, and deep as any that we have ever read. In construction, as well as in theology and in rhetoric, they are more than remarkable, and are amongst the best from his Grace's pen.'—*Union Review.*

The Prophet of Carmel: a Series of Practical Considerations upon the History of Elias in the Old Testament; with a Supplementary Dissertation. By the Rev. CHARLES B. GARSIDE, M.A.. Dedicated to the Very Rev. JOHN HENRY NEWMAN, D.D. 5*s.*

'There is not a page in these sermons but commands our respect. They are Corban in the best sense; they belong to the sanctuary, and are marked as divine property by a special cachet. They are simple without being trite, and poetical without being pretentious.'—*Westminster Gazette.*

'Full of spiritual wisdom uttered in pure and engaging language.'—The *Universe.*

'We see in these pages the learning of the divine, the elegance of the scholar, and the piety of the priest. Every point in the sacred narrative bearing upon the subject of his book is seized upon by the author with the greatest keenness of perception, and set forth with singular force and clearness.'—*Weekly Register.*

'Under his master-hand the marvellous career of the Prophet of Carmel displays its majestic proportions. His strong, nervous, incisive style has a beauty and a grace, a delicacy and a sensitiveness, that seizes hold of the heart and captivates the imagination. He has attained to the highest art of writing, which consists in selecting the words which express one's meaning with the greatest clearness in the least possible space.'—*Tablet.*

'The intellectual penetration, the rich imagination, the nervous eloquence which we meet with throughout the whole work, all combine to give it at once a very high place among the highest productions of our English Catholic literature.'—*Dublin Review.*

'Is at once powerful and engaging, and calculated to furnish ideas innumerable to the Christian preacher.'—*Church Review.*

'The thoughts are expressed in plain and vigorous English. The sermons are good specimens of the way in which Old Testament subjects should be treated for the instruction of a Christian congregation.'—*Church Times.*

Mary magnifying God: May Sermons. By the Rev. Fr. HUMPHREY, O.S.C. Cloth, 2*s.* 6*d.*

'Each sermon is a complete thesis, eminent for the strength of its logic, the soundness of its theology, and the lucidness of its expression. With equal force and beauty of language the author has provided matter for the most sublime meditations.'—*Tablet.*

'Dogmatic teaching of the utmost importance is placed before us so clearly, simply, and unaffectedly, that we find ourselves acquiring invaluable lessons of theology in every page.'—*Weekly Register.*

By the same,

The Divine Teacher. Second edition. 2*s.* 6*d.*

'The most excellent treatise we have ever read. It could not be clearer, and, while really deep, it is perfectly intelligible to any person of the most ordinary education.'—*Tablet.*

'We cannot speak in terms too high of the matter contained in this excellent and able pamphlet.'—*Westminster Gazette.*

Sermons by Fathers of the Society of Jesus.
Third edition. 7s.

CONTENTS : The Latter Days : Four Sermons by the Rev. H. J. Coleridge. The Temptations of our Lord : Four Sermons by the Rev. Father Hathaway. The Angelus Bell : Five Lectures on the Remedies against Desolation by the Very Rev. Father Gallwey, Provincial of the Society. The Mysteries of the Holy Infancy : Seven Sermons by Fathers Parkinson, Coleridge, and Harper.

Also, printed separately from above,

The Angelus Bell : Five Lectures on the
Remedies against Desolation. By the Very Rev. Father GALLWEY, Provincial of the Society of Jesus. 1s. 6d.

Also Vol. II. in same series,

Discourses by the Rev. Fr. Harper, S.J. 6s.
Also, just published, Vol. III. 6s.

CONTENTS : Sermons by the Rev. George R. Kingdon : I. What the Passion of Christ teaches us ; II. Our Lord's Agony in the Garden ; III. The Choice between Jesus and Barabbas ; IV. Easter Sunday (I.) ; V. Easter Sunday (II.) ; VI. Corpus Christi. Sermons by the Rev. Edward I. Purbrick : VII. Grandeur and Beauty of the Holy Eucharist ; VIII. Our Lady of Victories ; IX. The Feast of All Saints (I.) ; X. The Feast of All Saints (II.) ; XI. The Feast of the Immaculate Conception ; XII. The Feast of St. Joseph. Sermons by the Rev. Henry J. Coleridge : XIII. Fruits of Holy Communion (I.) ; XIV. Fruits of Holy Communion (II.) ; XV. Fruits of Holy Communion (III.) ; XVI. Fruits of Holy Communion (IV.). Sermons by the Rev. Alfred Weld : XVII. On the Charity of Christ ; XVIII. On the Blessed Sacrament. Sermons by the Rev. William H. Anderdon : XIX. The Corner-Stone a Rock of Offence ; XX. The Word of God heard or rejected by Men.

WORKS WRITTEN AND EDITED BY LADY GEORGIANA FULLERTON.

The Straw-cutter's Daughter, and the Por-
trait in my Uncle's Dining-room. Two Stories. Translated from the French. 2s. 6d.

Life of Luisa de Carvajal.   6s.

Seven Stories.   3s. 6d.

> CONTENTS: I. Rosemary: a Tale of the Fire of London.
> II. Reparation: a Story of the Reign of Louis XIV. III.
> The Blacksmith of Antwerp. IV. The Beggar of the Steps
> of St. Roch: a True Story. V. Trouvaille, or the Soldier's
> Adopted Child: a True Story. VI. Earth without Heaven:
> a Reminiscence. VII. Ad Majorem Dei Gloriam.

'Will well repay perusal.'—*Weekly Register.*
'Each story in this series has its own charm.'—*Tablet.*
'In this collection may be found stories sound in doctrine and intensely interesting as any which have come from the same pen.'—*Catholic Opinion.*
'As admirable for their art as they are estimable for their sound teaching.'—*Cork Examiner.*

A Sketch of the Life of the late Father Henry
Young, of Dublin.   2s. 6d.

Life of Mère Marie de la Providence,
Foundress of the Order of the 'Helpers of the Holy Souls.'

> The materials of this Biography have been drawn from
> the 'Notice sur la Révérende Mère Marie de la Providence,'
> published in Paris in 1872; the work of the Rev. Père Blôt,
> 'Les Auxiliatrices des Ames du Purgatoire;' and some ad-
> ditional documents furnished to the authoress by the Reli-
> gious of the Rue de la Barouillière.   2s.

Laurentia: a Tale of Japan.   Second edition.   3s. 6d.

'Has very considerable literary merit, and possesses an interest entirely its own. The dialogue is easy and natural, and the incidents are admirably grouped.'—*Weekly Register.*
'Full of romantic records of the heroism of the early Christians of Japan in the sixteenth century. Looking at its literary merits alone, it must be pronounced a really beautiful story.'—*Catholic Times.*

Life of St. Frances of Rome.   2s. 6d.; cheap
edition, 1s. 8d.

Rose Leblanc: a Tale of great interest.   3s.

Grantley Manor: the well-known and favourite
Novel.   Cloth, 3s. 6d.; cheap edition, 2s. 6d.

Germaine Cousin: a Drama.   6d.

Fire of London: a Drama.   6d.

OUR LADY'S BOOKS.

Uniformly printed in foolscap 8vo, limp cloth.

No. 1.

Memoir of the Hon. Henry E. Dormer. 2*s.*

No. 2.

Life of Mary Fitzgerald, a Child of the Sacred Heart. 2*s.*; cheap edition, 1*s.*

Meditations for every Day in the Year, and

for the Principal Feasts. By the Ven. Fr. NICHOLAS LANCICIUS, of the Society of Jesus. With Preface by the Rev. GEORGE PORTER, S.J. 6*s.* 6*d.*

'Most valuable, not only to religious, for whom they were originally intended, but to all those who desire to consecrate their daily life by regularly express and systematic meditation; while Father Porter's excellent little Preface contains many valuable hints on the method of meditation.'—*Dublin Review.*

'Full of Scripture, short and suggestive. The editor gives a very clear explanation of the Ignatian method of meditation. The book is a very useful one.'—*Tablet.*

'Short and simple, and dwell almost entirely on the life of our Blessed Lord, as related in the Gospels. Well suited to the wants of Catholics living in the world.'—*Weekly Register.*

'A book of singular spirituality and great depth of piety. Nothing could be more beautiful or edifying than the thoughts set forth for reflection, clothed as they are in excellent and vigorous English.'—*Union Review.*

Meditations for the Use of the Clergy, for

every Day in the Year, on the Gospels for the Sundays. From the Italian of Mgr. SCOTTI, Archbishop of Thessalonica. Revised and edited by the Oblates of St. Charles. With a Preface by his Grace the ARCHBISHOP OF WESTMINSTER.

Vol. I. From the First Sunday in Advent to the Sixth Saturday after the Epiphany. 4*s.*

Vol. II. From Septuagesima Sunday to the Fourth Sunday after Easter. 4*s.*

Vol. III. From the Fifth Sunday after Easter to the Eleventh Sunday after Pentecost. 4*s.*

Vol. IV., completing the work. 4*s.*

'This admirable little book will be much valued by all, but especially by the clergy, for whose use it is more immediately intended. The Archbishop states in his Preface that it is held in high esteem in Rome, and that he has himself found, by the experience of many years, its singular excellence, its practical piety, its abundance of Scripture, of the Fathers, and of ecclesiastical writers.'—*Tablet.*

'It is a sufficient recommendation to this book of meditations that our Archbishop has given them his own warm approval. . . . They are full of the language of the Scriptures, and are rich with unction of their Divine sense.'—*Weekly Register.*

'A manual of meditations for priests, to which we have seen nothing comparable.'—*Catholic World.*

'There is great beauty in the thoughts, the illustrations are striking, the learning shown in patristic quotation considerable, and the special applications to priests are very powerful. It is entirely a priest's book.'—*Church Review.*

The Question of Anglican Ordinations dis-

cussed. By the Very Rev. Canon ESTCOURT, M.A., F.A.S. With an Appendix of Original Documents and Photographic Facsimiles. One vol. 8vo, 14*s*.

'A valuable contribution to the theology of the Sacrament of Order. He treats a leading question, from a practical point of view, with great erudition, and with abundance of illustrations from the rites of various ages and countries.'—*Month.*

'Will henceforth be an indispensable portion of every priest's library, inasmuch as it contains all the information that has been collected in previous works, sifted and corrected, together with a well-digested mass of important matter which has never before been given to the public.'—*Tablet.*

'Marks a very important epoch in the history of that question, and virtually disposes of it.'—*Messenger.*

'Canon Estcourt has added valuable documents that have never appeared before, or never at full length. The result is a work of very great value.'—*Catholic Opinion.*

'Indicates conscientious and painstaking research, and will be indispensable to any student who would examine the question on which it treats.'—*Bookseller.*

'Superior, both in literary method, tone, and mode of reasoning, to the usual controversial books on this subject.'—*Church Herald.*

May Papers; or Thoughts on the Litanies of

Loreto. By EDWARD IGNATIUS PURBRICK, Priest of the Society of Jesus. 3*s.* 6*d.*

'There is a brightness and vivacity in them which will make them interesting to all, old and young alike, and adds to their intrinsic value.'—*Dublin Review.*

'We very gladly welcome this volume as a valuable addition to the now happily numerous manuals of devout exercises for the month.'—*Month.*

'Written in the pure, simple, unaffected language which becomes the subject.'—*Tablet.*

'We cannot easily conceive a book more calculated to aid the cause of true religion amongst young persons of every class.'—*Weekly Register.*

'They are admirable, and expressed in chaste and beautiful language. Although compiled in the first place for boys at school, they are adapted for the spiritual reading of Catholics of every age and condition of life.'—*Catholic Opinion.*

WORKS OF THE REV. FATHER RAWES, O.S.C.

Homeward: a Tale of Redemption. Second
edition. 3*s.* 6*d.*

'A series of beautiful word pictures.'—*Catholic Opinion.*
'A casket well worth the opening; full to the brim of gems of thought as beautiful as they are valuable.'—*Catholic Times.*
'Full of holy thoughts and exquisite poetry, and just such a book as can be taken up with advantage and relief in hours of sadness and depression.'—*Dublin Review.*
'Is really beautiful, and will be read with profit.'—*Church Times.*

God in His Works: a Course of Five Ser-
mons. 2*s.* 6*d.*

SUBJECTS: I. God in Creation. II. God in the Incarnation. III. God in the Holy See. IV. God in the Heart. V. God in the Resurrection.

'Full of striking imagery, and the beauty of the language cannot fail to make the book valuable for spiritual reading.'—*Catholic Times.*
'He has so applied science as to bring before the reader an unbroken course of thought and argument.'—*Tablet.*

The Beloved Disciple; or St. John the Evan-
gelist. 3*s.* 6*d.*

'Full of research, and of tender and loving devotion.'—*Tablet.*
'This is altogether a charming book for spiritual reading.'—*Catholic Times.*
'Through this book runs a vein of true, humble, fervent piety, which gives a singular charm.'—*Weekly Register.*
'St. John, in his varied character, is beautifully and attractively presented to our pious contemplation.'—*Catholic Opinion.*

Septem: Seven Ways of hearing Mass. Fifth
edition. 1*s.* and 2*s.*; red edges, 2*s.* 6*d.*; calf, 4*s.*; French Translation, 1*s.* 6*d.*

'A great assistance to hearing Mass with devotion. Besides its devotional advantages it possesses a Preface, in clear and beautiful language, well worth reading.'—*Tablet.*

Great Truths in Little Words. Third edi-
tion. Neat cloth, 3*s.* 6*d.*

'A most valuable little work. All may learn very much about the Faith rom it.'—*Tablet.*
'At once practical in its tendency, and elegant; oftentimes poetical in its diction.'—*Weekly Register.*
'Cannot fail to be most valuable to every Catholic; and we feel certain, when known and appreciated, it will be a standard work in Catholic households.'—*Catholic Times.*

A 2

Hymns, Original, &c.   Neat cloth, 1s.; cheap edition, 6d.

* *The Eucharistic Month.* From the Latin of Father LERCARI, S.J.   6d.; cloth, 1s.

* *Twelve Visits to our Lady and the Heavenly City of God.*   Second edition.   8d.

* *Nine Visits to the Blessed Sacrament.* Chiefly from the Canticle of Canticles.   Second edition.   6d.

* *Devotions for the Souls in Purgatory.* Second edition.   8d.

* Or in one vol.,

Visits and Devotions.   Neat cloth, 3s.

WORKS BY FATHER ANDERDON, S.J.

Christian Æsop.   3s. 6d. and 4s.

In the Snow : Tales of Mount St. Bernard. Sixth edition.   Cloth, 1s. 6d.

Afternoons with the Saints.   Eighth edition, enlarged.   5s.

Catholic Crusoe.   Seventh edition.   Cloth gilt, 3s. 6d.

Confession to a Priest.   1d.

What is the Bible ? Is yours the right Book ? New edition.   1d.

Also, edited by Father Anderdon,

What do Catholics really believe ?   2d.

Cherubini : Memorials illustrative of his Life. With Portrait and Catalogue of his Works.   By EDWARD BELLASIS, Barrister-at-Law.   One vol., 429 pp.   10s. 6d.

Louise Lateau of Bois d'Haine: her Life,

her Ecstasies, and her Stigmata: a Medical Study. By Dr. F. LEFEBVRE, Professor of General Pathology and Therapeutics in the Catholic University of Louvain, &c. Translated from the French. Edited by Rev. J. SPENCER NORTHCOTE, D.D. Full and complete edition. 3*s.* 6*d.*

'The name of Dr. Lefebvre is sufficient guarantee of the importance of any work coming from his pen. The reader will find much valuable information.'—*Tablet.*

'The whole case thoroughly entered into and fully considered. The Appendix contains many medical notes of interest.'—*Weekly Register.*

'A full and complete answer.'—*Catholic Times.*

Twelve New Tales. By Mrs. PARSONS.

1. Bertha's Three Fingers. 2. Take Care of Yourself. 3. Don't Go In. 4. The Story of an Arm-chair. 5. Yes and No. 6. The Red Apples under the Tree. 7. Constance and the Water Lilies. 8. The Pair of Gold Spectacles. 9. Clara's New Shawl. 10. The Little Lodgers. 11. The Pride and the Fall. 12. This Once.

3*d.* each ; in a Packet complete, 3*s.* ; or in cloth neat, 3*s.* 6*d.*

'Sound Catholic theology and a truly religious spirit breathes from every page, and it may be safely commended to schools and convents.'—*Tablet.*

'Full of sound instruction given in a pointed and amusing manner.'—*Weekly Register.*

'Very pretty, pleasantly told, attractive to little folks, and of such a nature that from each some moral good is inculcated. The tales are cheerful, sound, and sweet, and should have a large sale.'—*Catholic Times.*

'A very good collection of simple tales. The teaching is Catholic throughout.'—*Catholic Opinion.*

Marie and Paul: a Fragment. By 'Our

Little Woman.' 3*s.* 6*d.* ; gilt edges, 4*s.*

'We heartily recommend this touching little tale, especially as a present for children and for schools, feeling sure that none can rise from its perusal without being touched, both at the beauty of the tale itself and by the tone of earnest piety which runs through the whole, leaving none but holy thoughts and pleasant impressions on the minds of both old and young.'—*Tablet.*

'Well adapted to the innocent minds it is intended for. The little book would be a suitable present for a little friend.'—*Catholic Opinion.*

'A charming tale for young and old.'—*Cork Examiner.*

'To all who read it the book will suggest thoughts for which they will be the better, while its graceful and affecting, because simple, pictures of home and family life will excite emotions of which none need be ashamed.'—*Month.*

'Told effectively and touchingly, with all that tenderness and pathos in which gifted women so much excel.'—*Weekly Register.*

'A very pretty and pathetic tale.'—*Catholic World.*

'A very charming story, and may be read by both young and old.'—*Brownson's Review.*

'Presents us with some deeply-touching incidents of family love and devotion.'—*Catholic Times.*

Dame Dolores, or the Wise Nun of Easton-
mere ; and other Stories. By the Author of 'Tyborne,' &c. 4s.

CONTENTS: I. The Wise Nun of Eastonmere. II. Known Too Late. III. True to the End. IV. Olive's Rescue.

'We have read the volume with considerable pleasure, and we trust no small profit. The tales are decidedly clever, well worked out, and written with a flowing and cheerful pen.'—*Catholic Times.*

'The author of *Tyborne* is too well known to need any fresh recommendation to the readers of Catholic fiction. We need only say that her present will be as welcome to her many friends as any of her former works.'—*Month.*

'An attractive volume ; and we know of few tales that we can more safely or more thoroughly recommend to our young readers.'—*Weekly Register.*

Maggie's Rosary, and other Tales. By the
Author of 'Marian Howard.' Cloth extra, 3s., cheap edition, 2s.

'We strongly recommend these stories. They are especially suited to little girls.'—*Tablet.*

'The very thing for a gift-book for a child ; but at the same time so interesting and full of incident that it will not be contemned by children of a larger growth.'—*Weekly Register.*

'We have seldom seen tales better adapted for children's reading.'—*Catholic Times.*

'The writer possesses in an eminent degree the art of making stories for children.'—*Catholic Opinion,*

'A charming little book, which we can heartily recommend.'—*Rosarian.*

Scenes and Incidents at Sea. A new Selection. 1s. 4d.

CONTENTS : I. Adventure on a Rock. II. A Heroic Act of Rescue. III. Inaccessible Islands. IV. The Shipwreck of the Czar Alexander. V. Captain James's Adventures in the North Seas. VI. Destruction of Admiral Graves's Fleet. VII. The Wreck of the Forfarshire, and Grace Darling. VIII. The Loss of the Royal George. IX. The Irish Sailor Boy. X. Gallant Conduct of a French Privateer. XI. The Harpooner. XII. The Cruise of the Agamemnon. XIII. A Nova Scotia Fog. XIV. The Mate's Story. XV. The Shipwreck of the Æneas Transport. XVI. A Scene in the Shrouds. XVII. A Skirmish off Bermuda. XVIII. Charles Wager. XIX. A Man Overboard. XX. A Loss and a Rescue. XXI. A Melancholy Adventure on the American Seas. XXII. Dolphins and Flying Fish.

History of England, for Family Use and the

Upper Classes of Schools. By the Author of 'Christian Schools and Scholars.' Second edition. With Preface by the Very Rev. Dr. NORTHCOTE. 6s.

Tales from the Diary of a Sister of Mercy.

By C. M. BRAME. New edition. Cloth extra, 4s.

CONTENTS : The Double Marriage. The Cross and the Crown. The Novice. The Fatal Accident. The Priest's Death. The Gambler's Wife. The Apostate. The Besetting Sin.

'Written in a chaste, simple, and touching style.'—*Tablet.*
'This book is a casket, and those who open it will find the gem within.'—*Register.*
'They are well and cleverly told, and the volume is neatly got up.'—*Month.*
'Very well told : all full of religious allusions and expressions.'—*Star.*
'Very well written, and life-like ; many very pathetic.'—*Catholic Opinion*

By the same,

Angels' Visits: a Series of Tales. With

Frontispiece and Vignette. 3s. 6d.

'The tone of the book is excellent, and it will certainly make itself a great favourite with the young.'—*Month.*
'Beautiful collection of Angel Stories.'—*Weekly Register.*
'One of the prettiest books for children we have seen.'—*Tablet.*
'A book which excites more than ordinary praise.'—*Northern Press.*
'Touchingly written, and evidently the emanation of a refined and pious mind.'—*Church Times.*
'A charming little book, full of beautiful stories of the family of angels.'—*Church Opinion.*

ST. JOSEPH'S THEOLOGICAL LIBRARY.

Edited by Fathers of the Society of Jesus.

Vol. I.

On some Popular Errors concerning Politics and Religion. By the Right Honourable Lord ROBERT MONTAGU, M.P. 6s.

CONTENTS : Introduction. I. The Basis of Political Science. II. Religion. III. The Church. IV. Religious Orders. V. Christian Law. VI. The Mass. VII. The Principles of 1789. VIII. Liberty. IX. Fraternity. X. Equality. XI. Nationality, Non-intervention, and the Accomplished Fact. XII. Capital Punishment. XIII. Liberal Catholics.

XIV. Civil Marriage.   XV. Secularisation of Education. XVI. Conclusion.   Additional Notes.

This book has been taken from the 'Risposte popolari alle obiezioni piu diffuse contro la Religione; opera del P. Secondo Franco.   Torino, 1868.'   It is not a translation of that excellent Italian work, for much has been omitted, and even the forms of expression have not been retained ; nor yet is it an abstract, for other matter has been added throughout.   The aim of the editor has been merely to follow out the intention of P. Franco, and adapt his thoughts to the circumstances and mind of England.

Considerations for a Three Days' Preparation for Communion.

tion for Communion.   Taken chiefly from the French of SAINT JURE, S.J.   By CECILIE MARY CADDELL.   8*d.*

' In every respect a most excellent manual.'—*Catholic Times.*
'A simple and easy method for a devout preparation for that solemn duty.'—*Weekly Register.*
'A beautiful compilation carefully prepared.'—*Universe.*

The Spiritual Conflict and Conquest.

By Dom J. CASTANIZA, O.S.B.   Edited, with Preface and Notes, by Canon VAUGHAN, English Monk of the Order of St. Benedict.   Second edition.   Reprinted from the old English Translation of 1652.   With fine Original Frontispiece reproduced in Autotype.   8*s.* 6*d.*

The Letter-Books of Sir Amias Poulet,

Keeper of Mary Queen of Scots.   Edited by JOHN MORRIS, Priest of the Society of Jesus.   Demy 8vo, 10*s.* 6*d.*

Sir Amias Poulet had charge of the Queen of Scots from April 1585 to the time of her death, February 8, 1587. His correspondence with Lord-Treasurer Burghley and Sir Francis Walsingham enters into the details of her life in captivity at Tutbury, Chartley, and Fotheringay.   Many of the letters now published are entirely unknown, being printed from a recently-discovered manuscript.   The others have been taken from the originals at the Public Record Office and the British Museum.   The letters are strung together by a running commentary, in the course of which several of Mr. Froude's statements are examined, and the question of Mary's complicity in the plot against Elizabeth's life is discussed.

Sœur Eugenie: the Life and Letters of a
Sister of Charity. By the Author of 'A Sketch of the Life
of St. Paula.' Second edition, enlarged. On toned paper,
cloth gilt, 4s. 6d.; plain paper, cloth plain, 3s.

'It is impossible to read it without bearing away in one's heart some of
the "odour of sweetness" which breathes forth from almost every page.'—
Tablet.
'The most charming piece of religious biography that has appeared since
the *Récits d'une Sœur.'—Catholic Opinion.*
'We have seldom read a more touching tale of youthful holiness.'—*Weekly
Register.*
'The picture of a life of hidden piety and grace, and of active charity,
which it presents is extremely beautiful.'—*Nation.*
'We strongly recommend this devout and interesting life to the careful
perusal of all our readers.'—*Westminster Gazette.*

Count de Montalembert's Letters to a School-
fellow, 1827-1830. Qualis ab incepto. Translated from
the French by C. F. AUDLEY. With Portrait. 5s.

'Simple, easy, and unaffected in a degree, these letters form a really
charming volume. The observations are simply wonderful, considering that
when he wrote them he was only seventeen or eighteen years of age.'—
Weekly Register.
'A new treasure is now presented for the first time in an English casket—
the letters he wrote when a schoolboy. The loftiness of the aspirations they
breathe is supported by the intellectual power of which they give evidence.'
—*Cork Examiner.*
'Reveal in the future ecclesiastical champion and historian a depth of
feeling and insight into forthcoming events hardly to be expected from a
mere schoolboy.'—*Building News.*
'Display vigour of thought and real intellectual power.'—*Church Herald.*

Ecclesiastical Antiquities of London and its
Suburbs. By ALEXANDER WOOD, M.A. Oxon., of the So-
merset Archæological Society. 5s.

'O, who the ruine sees, whom wonder doth not fill
With our great fathers' pompe, devotion, and their skill?'

'Will prove a most useful manual to many of our readers. Stores of
Catholic memories still hang about the streets of this great metropolis. For
the ancient and religious associations of such places the Catholic reader can
want no better cicerone than Mr. Wood.'—*Weekly Register.*
'We have indeed to thank Mr. Wood for this excellent little book.'—
Catholic Opinion.
'Very seldom have we read a book devoted entirely to the metropolis
with such pleasure.'—*Liverpool Catholic Times.*
'A very pleasing and readable book.'—*Builder.*
'Gives a plain, sensible, but learned and interesting account of the chief
church antiquities of London and its suburbs. It is written by a very able
and competent author—one who thoroughly appreciates his subject, and
who treats it with the discrimination of a critic and the sound common sense
of a practised writer.'—*Church Herald.*

LIBRARY OF RELIGIOUS BIOGRAPHY.
Edited by EDWARD HEALY THOMPSON.

Vol. I.
The Life of St. Aloysius Gonzaga, S.J.
Second edition.   5s.

'Contains numberless traces of a thoughtful and tender devotion to the Saint. It shows a loving penetration into his spirit, and an appreciation of the secret motives of his action, which can only be the result of a deeply affectionate study of his life and character.'—*Month.*

Vol. II.
The Life of Marie Eustelle Harpain; or
the Angel of the Eucharist.   Second edition.   5s.

' Possesses a special value and interest apart from its extraordinay natural and supernatural beauty, from the fact that to her example and to the effect of her writings is attributed in great measure the wonderful revival of devotion to the Blessed Sacrament in France, and consequently throughout Western Christendom.'—*Dublin Review.*

'A more complete instance of that life of purity and close union with God in the world of which we have just been speaking is to be found in the history of Marie Eustelle Harpain, the sempstress of Saint-Pallais. The writer of the present volume has had the advantage of very copious materials in the French works on which his own work is founded ; and Mr. Thompson has discharged his office as editor with his usual diligence and accuracy.'—*Month.*

Vol. III.
The Life of St. Stanislas Kostka.   5s.

' We strongly recommend this biography to our readers.'—*Tablet.*

'There has been no adequate biography of St. Stanislas. In rectifying this want Mr. Thompson has earned a title to the gratitude of English-speaking Catholics. The engaging Saint of Poland will now be better known among us, and we need not fear that, better known, he will not be better loved.'—*Weekly Register.*

Vol. IV.
The Life of the Baron de Renty; or Per-
fection in the World exemplified.   6s.

' An excellent book. The style is throughout perfectly fresh and buoyant.'—*Dublin Review.*

'This beautiful work is a compilation, not of biographical incidents, but of holy thoughts and spiritual aspirations, which we may feed on and make our own.'—*Tablet.*

'Gives full particulars of his marvellous virtue in an agreeable form.'—*Catholic Times.*

' A good book for our Catholic young men, teaching how they can sanctify the secular state.'—*Catholic Opinion.*

' Edifying and instructive, a beacon and guide to those whose walks are in the ways of the world, who toil and strive to win Christian perfection.'—*Ulster Examiner.*

Vol. V.

The Life of the Venerable Anna Maria
Taigi, the Roman Matron (1769-1837). Third edition.
With Portrait. 6s.

This Biography has been written after a careful collation
of previous Lives of the Servant of God with each other,
and with the *Analecta Juris Pontificii,* which contain large
extracts from the Processes. Various prophecies attributed
to her and other holy persons have been collected in an
Appendix.

'Of all the series of deeply-interesting biographies which the untiring zeal
and piety of Mr. Healy Thompson has given of late years to English Catholics, none, we think, is to be compared in interest with the one before us,
both from the absorbing nature of the life itself and the spiritual lessons it
conveys.'—*Tablet.*

'A complete biography of the Venerable Matron in the composition of
which the greatest care has been taken and the best authorities consulted.
We can safely recommend the volume for the discrimination with which it
has been written, and for the careful labour and completeness by which it
has been distinguished.'—*Catholic Opinion.*

'We recommend this excellent and carefully-compiled biography to all
our readers. The evident care exercised by the editor in collating the
various lives of Anna Maria gives great value to the volume, and we hope it
will meet with the support it so justly merits.'—*Westminster Gazette.*

'We thank Mr. Healy Thompson for this volume. The direct purpose of
his biographies is always spiritual edification.'—*Dublin Review.*

'Contains much that is capable of nourishing pious sentiments.'—*Nation.*

'Has evidently been a labour of love.'—*Month.*

The Hidden Life of Jesus: a Lesson and
Model to Christians. Translated from the French of BOU-
DON, by EDWARD HEALY THOMPSON, M.A. Cloth, 3s.

'This profound and valuable work has been very carefully and ably translated by Mr. Thompson.'—*Register.*

'The more we have of such works as the *Hidden Life of Jesus* the better.'
—*Westminster Gazette.*

'A book of searching power.'—*Church Review.*

'We have often regretted that this writer's works are not better known.'
—*Universe.*

'We earnestly recommend its study and practice to all readers.'—*Tablet.*

'We have to thank Mr. Thompson for this translation of a valuable work
which has long been popular in France.'—*Dublin Review.*

'A good translation.'—*Month.*

Also, by the same Author and Translator,

Devotion to the Nine Choirs of Holy Angels,
and especially to the Angel Guardians. 3s.

'We congratulate Mr. Thompson on the way in which he has accomplished his task, and we earnestly hope that an increased devotion to the Holy Angels may be the reward of his labour of love.'—*Tablet.*
'A beautiful translation.'—*Month.*
'The translation is extremely well done.'—*Weekly Register.*

New Meditations for each Day in the Year,
on the Life of our Lord Jesus Christ. By a Father of the Society of Jesus. With the imprimatur of the Cardinal Archbishop of Westminster. New and improved edition. Two vols. Cloth, 9s.; also in calf, 16s.; morocco, 17s.

'We can heartily recommend this book for its style and substance ; it bears with it several strong recommendations. . . . It is solid and practical.' —*Westminster Gazette.*
'A work of great practical utility, and we give it our earnest recommendation.'—*Weekly Register.*

The Day Sanctified; being Meditations and
Spiritual Readings for Daily Use. Selected from the Works of Saints and approved Writers of the Catholic Church. Fcp. cloth, 3s. 6d.; red edges, 4s.

'Of the many volumes of meditations on sacred subjects which have appeared in the last few years, none has seemed to us so well adapted to its object as the one before us.'—*Tablet.*
'Deserves to be specially mentioned.'—*Month.*
'Admirable in every sense.'—*Church Times.*
'Many of the meditations are of great beauty. . . . They form, in fact, excellent little sermons, and we have no doubt will be largely used as such.' —*Literary Churchman.*

Reflections and Prayers for Holy Communion.
Translated from the French. With Preface by the CARDINAL ARCHBISHOP OF WESTMINSTER. Fcp. 8vo, cloth, 4s. 6d.; bound, red edges, 5s.; calf, 9s.; morocco, 10s.

'The Archbishop has marked his approval of the work by writing a preface for it, and describes it as "a valuable addition to our books of devotion."'—*Register.*
'A book rich with the choicest and most profound Catholic devotions.'— *Church Review.*

Lallemant's Doctrine of the Spiritual Life.
Edited by the late Father FABER. New edition. Cloth, 4*s.* 6*d.*

'This excellent work has a twofold value, being both a biography and a volume of meditations. It contains an elaborate analysis of the wants, dangers, trials, and aspirations of the inner man, and supplies to the thoughtful and devout reader the most valuable instructions for the attainment of heavenly wisdom, grace, and strength.'—*Catholic Times.*

'A treatise of the very highest value.'—*Month.*

'The treatise is preceded by a short account of the writer's life, and has had the wonderful advantage of being edited by the late Father Faber.'—*Weekly Register.*

The Rivers of Damascus and Jordan : a
Causerie. By a Tertiary of the Order of St. Dominic. 4*s.*

'Good solid reading.'—*Month.*

'Well done and in a truly charitable spirit.'—*Catholic Opinion.*

'It treats the subject in so novel and forcible a light that we are fascinated in spite of ourselves, and irresistibly led on to follow its arguments and rejoice at its conclusions.'—*Tablet.*

Legends of our Lady and the Saints ; or
our *Children's Book of Stories in Verse.* Written for the Recitations of the Pupils of the Schools of the Holy Child Jesus, St. Leonard's-on-Sea. 2*s.* 6*d.*

'It is a beautiful religious idea that is realised in the *Legends of our Lady and the Saints.* The book forms a charming present for pious children.'—*Tablet.*

'The "Legends" are so beautiful that they ought to be read by all lovers of poetry.'—*Bookseller.*

'Graceful poems.'—*Month.*

The New Testament Narrative, in the Words
of the Sacred Writers. With Notes, Chronological Tables, and Maps. Cloth, 2*s.*

'The compilers deserve great praise for the manner in which they have performed their task. We commend this little volume as well and carefully printed, and as furnishing its readers, moreover, with a great amount of useful information in the tables inserted at the end.'—*Month.*

'It is at once clear, complete, and beautiful.'—*Catholic Opinion.*

QUARTERLY SERIES.

Conducted by the Managers of the 'Month.'

———o———

VOLUMES PUBLISHED.

The Life and Letters of St. Francis Xavier.
By the Rev. H. J. COLERIDGE. Sec. edit. Two vols. 18s.

'We cordially thank Father Coleridge for a most valuable biography. . . . He has spared no pains to insure our having in good classical English a translation of all the letters which are extant. . . . A complete priest's manual might be compiled from them, entering as they do into all the details of a missioner's public and private life. . . . We trust we have stimulated our readers to examine them for themselves, and we are satisfied that they will return again and again to them as to a never-exhausted source of interest and edification.'—*Tablet*.

'A noble addition to our literature. . . . We offer our warmest thanks to Father Coleridge for this most valuable work. The letters, we need hardly say, will be found of great spiritual use, especially for missionaries and priests.'—*Dublin Review*.

'One of the most fascinating books we have met with for a long time.'—*Catholic Opinion*.

'Would that we had many more lives of saints like this! Father Cole-ridge has done great service to this branch of Catholic literature, not simply by writing a charming book, but especially by setting others an example of how a saint's life should be written.'—*Westminster Gazette*.

'This valuable book is destined, we feel assured, to take a high place among what we may term our English Catholic classics. . . . The great charm lies in the letters, for in them we have, in a far more forcible manner than any biographer could give them, the feelings, experiences, and aspira-tions of St. Francis Xavier as pictured by his own pen.'—*Catholic Times*.

'Father Coleridge does his own part admirably, and we shall not be sur-prised to find his book soon take its place as the standard Life of the saintly and illustrious Francis.'—*Nation*.

'Not only an interesting but a scholarly sketch of a life remarkable alike in itself and in its attendant circumstances. We hope the author will con-tinue to labour in a department of literature for which he has here shown his aptitude. To find a saint's life which is at once moderate, historical, and appreciative is not a common thing.'—*Saturday Review*.

'Should be studied by all missionaries, and is worthy of a place in every Christian library.'—*Church Herald*.

The Life of St. Jane Frances Fremyot de

Chantal. By EMILY BOWLES. With Preface by the Rev.
H. J. COLERIDGE. Second edition. 5*s.* 6*d.*

'We venture to promise great pleasure and profit to the réader of this
charming biography. It gives a complete and faithful portrait of one of the
most attractive saints of the generation which followed the completion of
the Council of Trent.'—*Month.*

'Sketched in a life-like manner, worthy of her well-earned reputation as
a Catholic writer.'—*Weekly Register.*

'We have read it on and on with the fascination of a novel, and yet it is
the life of a saint, described with a rare delicacy of touch and feeling such
as is seldom met with.'—*Tablet.*

'A very readable and interesting compilation. . . . The author has done
her work faithfully and conscientiously.'—*Athenæum.*

'Full of incident, and told in a style so graceful and felicitous that it wins
upon the reader with every page.'—*Nation.*

'Miss Bowles has done her work in a manner which we cannot better
commend than by expressing a desire that she may find many imitators.
She has endued her materials with life, and clothed them with a language
and a style of which we do not know what to admire most—the purity, the
grace, the refinement, or the elegance. If our readers wish to know the
value and the beauty of this book, they can do no better than get it and
read it.'—*Westminster Gazette.*

'One of the most charming and delightfu volumes which has issued from
the press for many years. Miss Bowles has accomplished her task faithfully
and happily, with simple grace and unpretentious language, and a winning
manner which, independently of her subject, irresistibly carries us along.'—
Ulster Examiner.

The History of the Sacred Passion. From

the Spanish of Father LUIS DE LA PALMA, of the Society
of Jesus. The Translation revised and edited by the Rev.
H. J. COLERIDGE. Third edition. 7*s.* 6*d.*

'A work long held in great and just repute in Spain. It opens a mine of
wealth to one's soul. Though there are many works on the Passion in English, probably none will be found so generally useful both for spiritual reading and meditation. We desire to see it widely circulated.'—*Tablet.*

'A sterling work of the utmost value, proceeding from the pen of a great
theologian, whose piety was as simple and tender as his learning and culture
were profound and exquisite. It is a rich storehouse for contemplation on
the great mystery of our Redemption, and one of those books which every
Catholic ought to read for himself.'—*Weekly Register.*

'The most wonderful work upon the Passion that we have ever read. To
us the charm lies in this, that it is entirely theological. It is made use of
largely by those who give the Exercises of St. Ignatius; it is, as it were,
the flesh upon the skeleton of the Exercises. Never has the Passion been
meditated upon so before. . . . If any one wishes to understand the Passion
of our Lord in its fulness, let him procure this book.'—*Dublin Review.*

'We have not read a more thoughtful work on our Blessed Lord's Passion.

It is a complete storehouse of matter for meditation, and for sermons on that divine mystery.'—*Catholic Opinion.*

' The book is—speaking comparatively of human offerings—a magnificent offering to the Crucified, and to those who wish to make a real study of the Cross will be a most precious guide.'—*Church Review.*

Ierne of Armorica : a Tale of the Time of Chlovis. By J. C. BATEMAN. 6*s.* 6*d.*

' We know of few tales of the kind that can be ranked higher than the beautiful story before us. The author has hit on the golden mean between an over-display of antiquarianism and an indolent transfer of modern modes of action and thought to a distant time. The descriptions are masterly, the characters distinct, the interest unflagging. We may add that the period is one of those which may be said to be comparatively unworked.'—*Month.*

' A volume of very great interest and very great utility. As a story it is sure to give much delight, while, as a story founded on historical fact, it will benefit all by its very able reproduction of very momentous scenes. . . . The book is excellent. If we are to have a literature of fiction at all, we hope it will include many like volumes.'—*Dublin Review.*

' Although a work of fiction, it is historically correct, and the author portrays with great skill the manners and customs of the times of which he professes to give a description. In reading this charming tale we seem to be taken by the hand by the writer, and made to assist at the scenes which he describes.'—*Tablet.*

' The author of this most interesting tale has hit the happy medium between a display of antiquarian knowledge and a mere reproduction in distant ages of commonplace modern habits of thought. The descriptions are excellent, the characters well drawn, and the subject itself is very attractive, besides having the advantage of not having been written threadbare.'—*Westminster Gazette.*

' The tale is excessively interesting, the language appropriate to the time and rank of the characters, the style flowing and easy, and the narrative leads one on and on until it becomes a very difficult matter to lay the book down until it is finished. . . . It is a valuable addition to Catholic fictional literature.'—*Catholic Times.*

' A very pretty historico-ecclesiastical novel of the times of Chlovis. It is full of incident, and is very pleasant reading.'—*Literary Churchman.*

The Life of Dona Luisa de Carvajal. By Lady GEORGIANA FULLERTON. 6*s.* (See p. 6.)

The Life of the Blessed John Berchmans. By the Rev. FRANCIS GOLDIE, S.J. 6*s.*

' A complete and life-like picture, and we are glad to be able to congratulate Father Goldie on his success.'—*Tablet.*

' Drawn up with a vigour and freedom which show great power of biographical writing.'—*Dublin Review.*

' One of the most interesting of all.'—*Weekly Register.*

' Unhesitatingly we say that it is the very best Life of Blessed John

Berchmans, and as such it will take rank with religious biographies of the highest merit.'—*Catholic Times.*

'Is of great literary merit, the style being marked by elegance and a complete absence of redundancy.'—*Cork Examiner.*

'This delightful and edifying volume is of the deepest interest. The perusal will afford both pleasure and profit.'—*Church Herald.*

The Life of the Blessed Peter Favre, of the

Society of Jesus, First Companion of St. Ignatius Loyola. From the Italian of Father GIUSEPPE BOERO, of the same Society. With Preface by the Rev. H. J. COLERIDGE. 6s. 6d.

This Life has been written on the occasion of the beatification of the Ven. Peter Favre, and contains the *Memoriale* or record of his private thoughts and meditations, written by himself.

'At once a book of spiritual reading, and also an interesting historical narrative. The *Memoriale, or Spiritual Diary*, is here translated at full length, and is the most precious portion of one of the most valuable biographies we know.'—*Tablet.*

'A perfect picture drawn from the life, admirably and succinctly told. The *Memoriale* will be found one of the most admirable epitomes of sound devotional reading.'—*Weekly Register.*

'The *Memoriale* is hardly excelled in interest by anything of the kind now extant.'—*Catholic Times.*

'Full of interest, instruction, and example.'—*Cork Examiner.*

'One of the most interesting to the general reader of the entire series up to this time.'—*Nation.*

'This wonderful diary, the *Memoriale*, has never been published before, and we are much mistaken if it does not become a cherished possession to thoughtful Catholics.'—*Month.*

The Dialogues of St. Gregory the Great.

An old English version. Edited, with Preface, by the Rev. H. J. COLERIDGE. 6s.

'The Catholic world must feel grateful to Father Coleridge for this excellent and compendious edition. The subjects treated of possess at this moment a special interest. . . . The Preface by Father Coleridge is interesting and well written, and we cordially recommend the book to the perusal of all.'—*Tablet.*

'This is a most interesting book. . . . Father Coleridge gives a very useful preface summarising the contents.'—*Weekly Register.*

'We have seldom taken up a book in which we have become at once so deeply interested. It will suit any one; it will teach all; it will confirm any who require that process; and it will last and be read when other works are quite forgotten.'—*Catholic Times.*

'Edited and published with the utmost care and the most perfect literary taste, this volume adds one more gem to the treasury of English Catholic literature.'—*New York Catholic World.*

The Life of Sister Anne Catherine Emme-
rich. Edited, with Preface, by the Rev. H. J. COLERIDGE.
5*s.*

St. Winefride; or Holywell and its Pil-
grims. By the Author of 'Tyborne.' Third edition. 1*s.*

Summer Talks about Lourdes. By Miss
CADDELL. Cloth, 1*s.* 6*d.*

Blessed Margaret Mary Alacoque: a brief
and popular Account of her Life; to which are added
Selections from some of her Sayings, and the Decree of her
Beatification. By the Rev. CHARLES B. GARSIDE, M.A.
1*s.*

A Comparison between the History of the
Church and the Prophecies of the Apocalypse. Translated
from the German by EDWIN DE LISLE. 2*s.*

CATHOLIC-TRUTH TRACTS.

NEW ISSUES.

Manchester Dialogues. First Series. By the
Rev. Fr. HARPER, S.J.

> No. I. The Pilgrimage.
> II. Are Miracles going on still?
> III. Popish Miracles tested by the Bible.
> IV. Popish Miracles.
> V. Liquefaction of the Blood of St. Januarius.
> VI. 'Bleeding Nuns' and 'Winking Madonnas.'
> VII. Are Miracles physically possible?
> VIII. Are Miracles morally possible?

Price of each 3*s.* per 100, 25 for 1*s.*; also 25 of the above
assorted for 1*s.* Also the whole Series complete in neat Wrap-
per, 6*d.*

Specimen Packet of General Series, containing 100 assorted,
1*s.* 6*d.*

www.ingramcontent.com/pod-product-compliance
Lightning Source LLC
Chambersburg PA
CBHW020040030726
47499CB00007B/2514